The Ali Files

The Ali Files

On the Town with Ali Akbar

Bill McGowan

CELTIC CAT PUBLISHING
Knoxville, Tennessee
2015

The stories: "The Jockey," "The Red Suit," "Donald Trump," "Ali's Birthday," "Suicide Watch," "That Means You Love Me," and "Twenty Dollars" originally appeared in *La Cuadra.* www.lacuadraonline.com

Soul Man by Ali Akbar (back cover) courtesy of Janie Minor
Rooster by Ali Akbar (pg. v) courtesy of Birgitta Barth
Front cover photo by Bill McGowan
Author photo by Luis Fernando Noriega

The Ali Files: On the Town with Ali Akbar / Bill McGowan
Illustrated by Luis De León Diaz

ISBN: 9780990594567

Celtic Cat Publishing
Knoxville, Tennessee
CelticCatPublishing.com

PCN: 2015938546

Printed in the United States of America
Sustainable Forestry Initiative® Certified Sourcing

Rooster, a self portrait

Contents

Introduction

Bill McGowan is a natural storyteller, and an excellent, soulful writer. This is a quality that we all, including himself, have only recently discovered, because after all the adventurous turns in his life he has only recently put his hand to writing. This new endeavor was fully precipitated by his late friend, the artist and poet, Ali Akbar, a.k.a. Horace Pittman. Ali passed away in 2009, and for the last few years of his life he and Bill were close friends and running buddies in the kind of cultural adventures that had always been part of Ali's life.

Bill and myself and so many others have long admired Ali for not only his art but also his rich and exuberant personality. His art was a bold and uninhibited expression, known for its provocative use of color, and this mirrors his life and character. One can't help but recall William Blake's oft repeated phrase "Exuberance is Beauty" when thinking of Ali. As Ali once said in a poem of his, "I love you in every color with a love that paints my world."

I believe most of these stories were written while Bill lived in Guatemala tending a used bookstore and contributing to a local magazine, *La Cuadra*. But the stories are set in Knoxville, Tennessee, with a few excursions outside that area, such as Ali's last big road trip to the nation's capitol with Bill. Ali spent most of the last half of his 64 years in Knoxville, becoming a notable and much loved figure in the art scene and around town. A retrospective exhibition of his work is scheduled to open in Knoxville this May of 2015, and this exceptional collection of stories will be one of the artifacts that accompany it.

RB Morris
Knoxville, TN
March 14, 2015

--- Original message ---
From: ali akhbar
To: Bill
Subject: Yangshuo, China
Date: Mon, 7 Jan 2008 00:55:57 -0800 (PST)

WOW!!!

Yes, this is very interesting, Chicago!!! It reads
like something out of an adventure novel or a movie.
I do know the book, "Blink" by Malcolm Gladwell. I
saw him on TV speaking on that book a couple times
or so. Have'nt read it yet. But, i did get it (what
he was saying)! You seem to pretty much be among
the people. I can see them being comfortable talk
with you because you are that kind of guy. And, you
know something about their Country.
    Keep up your writings man, that's your ART
FORM!!! You are out there, in the field man, down
in the trenches dude!!! Get the "WORD" for us
and bring it back. Then, you can write the book,
sell it and go back there and live "RICH":))!!!
BITCH!!!:))
    WOW!!! I was about to close out this email
when i realized (when reading your journal) i an
pictureing South Vietnam in my mind, and you are
in China!!! Black and White!!! Well, at least i
have some clue. Guest thats how i can relate, to
a degree, to your experiences there.
    Your description of the winter sun is so poetic:
"But it looked like the sun was shining again,
a rare occasion in China in the winter."

The Ali Files

The Jockey

One day Ali and I were sitting around shootin' the breeze, telling stories and drinking beer. The topic drifted to the natural beauty of the hills and mountains around Knoxville. Ali said he loved getting out into the mountains—like he had done one day with me and Herbie when we'd gone hiking in the Smokies.

But he added in his drawl, "Beel, I don't like going out to redneck areas around the South. It makes me too nervous."

"Well sure, Ali. But it's not as though you're going to drift into a cement-block bar in Cocke County or anything by mistake."

"No, Bill. But I don't even like going out Chapman Highway! In fact, that reminds me of a story."

Ali had many stories.

"There was this friend of mine," says Ali. "He was a white guy I was buying my weed from. One day he asked me if I wanted to go with him on the buy.

I said, 'Sure, where to?' When he told me it was out Chapman Highway, I changed my mind quick. I said, 'No way, man!'

"But he convinced me it would be okay. We'd just stop into this one house a block off the highway, pick up the weed, and be on our way in a few minutes. I said, 'Well, okay. I guess so.' But I was still pretty uncomfortable with the whole idea.

"Anyway, he was driving this late model Lincoln with fancy hubcaps. It was a pimp-mobile if I ever saw one. I kept my profile down all the way out Chapman Highway. I don't even like the idea of the people who live out there seeing a black guy cruising around their neck of the woods.

"We got to the house and he said I should come on in. That wasn't part of the deal, but I figured it would be even worse if I was sitting in that honky car all by myself in a white neighborhood. So, damn it, we went in. Turns out they were real nice people. We sat around smokin' some weed, and drinkin' some beers for awhile.

"When it got time to go, we said our goodbyes and got in the car. It was dusk. I was happy we were heading back in the dark. My friend pulled out of the driveway and started down the street. Then he suddenly stopped the car, jumped out, and I thought, 'What the hell is he doing?'

"I watched him run over to someone's front yard. They had one of those black lawn jockeys you used to see all over the South. He grabbed it out of the lawn and ran back to the car with it."

"I yelled at him, 'Man, you tryin' to get me killed? You know it's me who they're going to kill don't you?'

"He just laughed, hit the gas and away we went down the highway. Man, Bill, I thought it was all over. Weed in the car, and now a theft. I was pissed. But you know, the farther we got away from there and the closer we got to Knoxville, the better I felt. I looked in the backseat. He was standing back there with that jet-black face and that stupid smile, holding out those reins. And I felt like we had rescued him.

"Well, we got back to Knoxville. I asked my friend to drop me off at the Long Branch. By this time I was feeling good—like I was a Liberator. I got out of the car and took the jockey with me. I composed myself, and walked into the Long Branch with him under my arm. When I hit the door everyone looked up to see me, expecting my usual loud entry. I didn't say a word and didn't crack a smile. Everyone was looking at me. There wasn't a sound. I walked over to the bar, stood the jockey on the bar and said, 'I'll have a PBR—and get one for my friend, too.'

"That's how it was the whole night too, Bill. No one asked me a thing. I just drank the whole night there with that full beer sittin' in front of that damn jockey."

The Red Suit

I had the benefit of hearing this story twice. Ali told it to me once, and then I got to hear him tell it to an unknown couple that we invited to sit at our table in some bar a few years later. I realized with the second telling that Ali had refined this story over the years to achieve maximum effect.

"After I got back from 'Nam, I went back home to Rock Hill, South Carolina. I couldn't stand it. It seemed so small to me after having been in Vietnam and then San Francisco. I was getting on the nerves of my family and they were sure botherin' me. I couldn't relate to anyone, even my old high school buddies. And I realized it wasn't going to be easy with the women either.

"I had this uncle that was only about fifteen years older than me that lived up in New Jersey. I'd always looked up to him. He had a reputation as a real ladies' man. My mother suggested I go visit him for a while. That sounded like a great idea to me! He invited me up there to stay with him.

"Hey, Uncle Joe was living good. He had a decent job, money in his pocket, many women. He was a dresser. He knew just about everyone in town. He took me around to all of his haunts and even found me a part-time job. I was tryin' to model myself on him, learning the way; I always had the jive.

"At this time he was livin' with a really hot babe. Man, Jessie was sharp! One day I got home from work around six in the evening. I was dead tired. No one was home, so I decided to lie down on my uncle's bed. I was tired of always sleeping on the couch. I figured I'd get up as soon as someone came home.

"I fell asleep. When Jessie came home she went to the bathroom, and then came straight into the bedroom thinking it was my uncle in there. I woke up when she laid down next to me with next to nothin' on. It was dark. It was crazy, but I couldn't resist just goin' with the flow. Well, we were playing around and I was just about to go IN there when the front door opened.

"My uncle called out, 'Hey, where is everybody?'

"The gig was up!

"She jumped up, turned the light on, and said, 'What the fuck are you doin in the bed, Horace?'"

(Horace was his given name. He took Ali Akbar later, when he converted to Islam.)

"Man, she was pissed. She started screamin' at

me, and then she went out to my uncle complainin' about what I'd done to her.

"My uncle called me out gruffly, 'Horace, get your ass out here!'

"I got my clothes on, and came out to the living room.

"He laid into me. I tried to apologize and say it was just an accident. The whole time she was still yellin' at me and telling my uncle he needed to kick me out of the house.

"'Horace, you heard her. Man, you got to go. And NOW!'

"I gathered up my clothes and stuff and packed them in my bag. I didn't have much. I walked out, saying I was sorry again. I didn't know where the hell to go, so I just walked down the block to a little tavern we always went to.

"I was well on my way to my sixth or seventh drink when my uncle walked in. Man, I jumped up. I was real nervous. He walked up to me.

"'Uncle Joe, I'm real sorry about what happened,' I said.

"I wasn't sure he wouldn't hit me. He was a big man! He surprised the hell out of me when he walked up and put his big arm around my shoulder.

"Laughing, he said, 'Oh Horace, don't worry about that. I just had to kick you out because she was so mad. I've called your Auntie; you can stay with her a few days. Then you can come back to my place after Jessie calms down.'

"'Boy,' he added, 'I can't believe you pulled that stunt! Let me buy you a drink.'

"That's the way my uncle was. He taught me a lot."

"After a few months up there, I had a little money in my pocket. I had my own apartment then. I knew I needed some good clothes. My uncle dressed well, and I saw the effect that had on everyone, particularly the ladies. So I went to this men's clothing shop in the 'hood and I bought a nice suit. Fitted! Red! That night I hit the clubs in my suit and a nice hat too. Wow! I felt like the MAN. I could feel the effect immediately. It gave me confidence, and I played it for all it was worth.

"The first time my uncle saw me in the suit, I think he was a little jealous. You know, he was a little older, and here was this young upstart that he had helped gettin' all of the attention. Still, he was cordial to me. And, you know, I was always glad to see him.

"I hung out up there in Jersey for a year or two. Even stayed for a while in New York City. But eventually, I ran out of jobs and money, and decided to go back home to Rock Hill. That was disappointing, to say the least. I was even more

disconnected than before. I couldn't find work.
I was living at home. The scene there was sooo
small-town. I'll never forget, and maybe never
forgive, that my mother at this time suggested I try
to get a job on a garbage truck! A garbage truck!!!
Whoa, that's what she thought I should aspire to?"

"After about six months in Rock Hill, I thought I
might as well go back to San Francisco. When I was
stationed there, it was the most exciting place I'd
ever lived. I pulled together enough bread to catch a
bus out there. I was big-time broke but, you know,
I found my way. I was livin' over in Oakland where
it was cheap, and makin' my way over to the City
as often as I could.

"Before long, I started picking up a little dough
sellin' weed, and pretty soon I'd built up a clientele.

"One day I was standing on my corner where I
knew some people would find me. I had the weed
in my pocket.

"Suddenly a cop car pulled up and they jumped
out. They asked me to empty my pockets and there
it was. There was no gettin' out of it. They arrested
me and put me in the back of the car. I was had.
There was no point in arguing. I was goin' in.

"A white cop was driving. His partner was black.
They weren't bad; weren't mean to me at all. I was
sittin' back there, kinda calm. I asked them, 'Hey,

you got me fair and square. But what I can't figure is how you knew to pick ME up.

"They looked at each other and smiled. The black cop turned to me and said, 'We got a tip!'

"'What tip?' I asked.

"They looked at each other again, smiling. The black cop turned to me again, and almost laughin' said, 'The nigger in the red suit gots the dope!'

"Even I had to laugh at that!"

Donald Trump

I picked up Ali one night at his crib. We were going out to hear some music. He was in a great mood when he got in the car. And he was dressed to the nines. He relayed this story to me about what had just happened to him about two hours ago.

"Hey Chicago! Wassup?"

That was one of his nicknames for me: "Chicago."

"You're looking good, Ali." I said.

"Bill, you won't believe what happened to me this afternoon. You won't believe what I had to go through to get this outfit together for tonight."

"Tell me about it, Ali."

"Well, Bill, I was getting dressed about three hours ago. This is a special occasion tonight and I wanted to look my best. Hey, we're going to see my boy, RB, at the Laurel! I want to show him some respect. I had the outfit just about together, but I discovered I was missing something. 'Oh well,' I thought, 'I've got time to walk on down to the Goodwill and pick up what I need.' You know I do most of my shopping there. So, I headed out and was walking down that cutoff between Sutherlin Ave. to Kingston Pike. It was a nice summer evening. I was feeling good. Then I spotted this patrol car coming down the cutoff toward me. And I noticed it was going real slow. As it got closer I could see the officer was a female and she was eyeballing me as I walked.

"'Here we go,' I thought.

"I kept on walking with my eyes straight ahead. A minute or two later and here she comes again, this time in my direction. She's passing me and slowing down. I ignored it, and kept on walking. I watched the car pull ahead of me again and then turn into a parking lot beside me and stop. The police lady got out of the car and started walking across the lot in a beeline right towards me. I got to that point where we'd meet . . . and I just kept on walking past her.

"She said, 'Aren't you going to talk to me?'

"I stopped, turned to her and said, 'Well, noooo, officer. I wasn't planning on talking with you, but apparently, You are going to talk to me.'

"She said, 'We have a report of a person causing a disturbance at Goodwill, and I'd like to talk to you about that.'

"Bill, without a moment's hesitation, I replied, 'Officer, what exactly is it about me that makes you

think I buy my clothes at Goodwill?'

"She hesitated a moment, not knowing how to reply . . . then I said, 'I mean, if I were Donald Trump walking down this street, would you ask me if I frequented Goodwill?'

"She stammered, tripping over whatever reply she could come up with.

"And then I turned and walked away, right down the sidewalk in the direction of Goodwill. She never said another word to me. And when I got there, I picked up this great scarf. And that's what makes this outfit.

"Hey Chicago, let's stop and get a drink before the show. I'm feeling good tonight!"

Ali's Birthday

The first couple of years that I knew Ali Akbar, we were only casual friends. Usually, I'd run into him when visiting someone we both knew or when we both were in the same bar and the same time. We always hit it off, but it wasn't until about 2001 that I started running around with him regularly.

He called me one night, back in about 2002.

"Hey, Ali, what's going on?" I answered the phone.

"Bill, it's my birthday this Friday. Do you want to go out for a few beers?"

"Damn, that's great. Um . . . Well . . . Happy Birthday in advance!" I replied.

I was stalling for time on the request, because, in fact, I wasn't sure if I wanted to go out with Ali for his birthday. Or, maybe more to the point, I was afraid to. I'd already been with him on a number of occasions when his antics spoiled the night. I'd been with him and cleaned up the mess after he'd gotten drunk and eighty-sixed from several joints around town. If he was celebrating his birthday, I figured, then he'd probably be hitting it hard. I'm not used to getting kicked out of bars. It's happened, of course, but mostly when I was in my twenties. But back in the early 2000s, I was in a professional mode and it embarrassed me a little to be a party to something like that.

Still, regardless of my best intentions, I heard myself saying, "Sure, Ali. It will be a blast."

I had my trepidations, but it was a birthday request from Ali. How could I turn that down?

I picked Ali up about six in the evening. He wanted to get an early start. We headed out to Baker Peters Jazz and Blues Club. It was pretty far out west in Knoxville. I seldom headed out that way, but Ali knew the band that was playing, and he jumped right in to the music. I suspected that he may have started drinking long before I tooted the horn outside his apartment. Man, he was wound up! He was getting down right in front of the band. This was Ali, and they were friends, so there was no problem at all.

The management, on the other hand, didn't know what to make of Ali and they looked guardedly alarmed by his antics. Truth be told, the farther west you go in Knoxville, the whiter and uptighter it becomes. In old-school Tennessee, that combination brings out the bad in some white folks, particularly when a black man is having too good a time on "their turf," and things can get touch-and-go, real quick.

Ali was pretty well clued into such tensions, and we bailed just before it looked like we were going to be asked to leave.

As we hit the street, Ali said, "Let's head down to Cha-Cha's"

Cha-Cha's is in Bearden, a neighborhood on the more comfortable side of town for me and Ali. They often featured live jazz, and that night Donald Brown, one of our favorites, was playing. Donald Brown is a famed keyboard player in Knoxville who teaches in the Jazz program at the University of Tennessee. At Cha-Cha's, the bar is in the front room; the music is in the back. We arrived early and having a bit of time to kill, we ordered a few beers and sat at the bar. The bar is small and takes a right angle, with no more than four stools on each wing.

Ali was flying high and I was rapidly catching up. I sat at the corner and Ali was next to me along one wing of the bar. On the other wing, a middle-aged couple were nursing cocktails. They looked like they had come into town from the west side. The woman was fascinated with Ali, who was fully animated, pulling laughter from those around him. The guy steadfastly ignored us. He seemed more than a little uncomfortable.

Ali was telling me stories, and jiving the staff. He knew the bar and restaurant workers pretty well, as he was a regular customer. The staff obviously knew him, enough that they loved his company, but also to know things could go south, and Ali was on a beautiful, drunken tear. He told them it was his birthday, so I think they were willing to cut him a little extra slack.

At some point, while he was telling me a story that had me in stitches, the woman on the other wing of the bar became more and more enchanted with Ali, leaning across the corner past me. When Ali stopped to take a breath in mid-story, she smiled and said, "I'd love to hear the story of how you lost your two front teeth."

I cringed, expecting the worst. The bartender heard the question and went on high alert, too. Ali had lost his two front teeth to dental problems within the last year. It wasn't a great story or anything, he just never had enough money for dental work and he was sensitive about it. I couldn't believe a stranger would ask such an insensitive question. The man could put on a show, but he sure as hell wasn't an act. Still, to her credit, the woman seemed to have no sense of it being insensitive. Maybe she was just so interested in Ali, that she seized on the first thing that came to mind.

Ali was less charitable in that passing moment.

"You want to know how I lost my front teeth?" he growled with indignation. "I'll tell you how I lost my front teeth, bitc—"

Before he could get the whole word out, her husband, suddenly aware of the situation and having a role to play, countered, "I don't believe you just called my wife a bitch!"

He looked like he was ready to knock Ali on his ass.

In the few seconds this all occurred, the bartender, seeing where it was heading, sent a waiter to get the boss, who came running out of the back room to head off the fight. He immediately asked Ali and me to leave. Ali was in such a good mood that he didn't make a fuss about it. We vacated the locale quickly. As we left, I glanced back and saw that the husband and wife were arguing with each other vociferously.

Ali thought what had just happened was hilarious. By the time we got outside, he was beside himself in convulsions of laughter. He fell down in the parking lot, grabbing his sides and trying to get control of himself. I took his hand and was trying to get him up, but he wasn't budging.

Now we were both laughing.

That was when Karly, one of our friends from around town, appeared out of nowhere in the park-

ing lot. She walked up to us, and said, incredulously, "What are you guys doing?"

She seemed embarrassed for us. She was right to
be, two grown men, one laying down in the middle
of a parking lot, laughing their asses off, obviously
more than a few drinks into the night, in the middle
of a major American city in the early 21st Century.
We must have looked like ten kinds of fool.

"Hey, Karly. We're alright," said Ali. "I just fell
down here in the parking lot because I was laughing
so hard."

"Well, what's so funny?" asked Karly.

Ali and I looked at each other and burst out laughing again. Then Ali said, by way of explanation, "It's
my birthday today, is all. Bill and I are celebrating."

"Whatever you say," Karly replied, loosening up
a little and laughing. "But maybe you should try
to keep on your feet. And stay out of trouble, too!"
she added.

"Sure Karly, good advice," said Ali, giggling as he
got back up with some help from me.

Once Karly had cleared the scene, and we'd gotten
hold of one another, Ali said, "Bill, let's bop into
4620. It's right down the road, and they might have
some jazz tonight. I'm in the mood for some jazz
and we never got to hear note one at Cha-Cha's."

"Sounds good to me, Ali," I responded, and off
we went.

The 4620 Club is a great music venue. It is in the basement, down a long flight of stairs, in an otherwise nondescript strip mall. Ali was very well known there, too. In fact, he'd been kicked out of that club more times in the short time it had been open, than anywhere else in town! Yet, he was a good customer, too.

That incongruity was an essential Ali feature. His behavior often got him in trouble with people, but at the same time, even with the same person, his zest for life was so infectious that folks wanted to know him anyway. They wanted him around. At the 4620, they liked Ali, but they had developed a low tolerance for any over-the-top behavior. It was a jazz and blues club. Cats needed to be cool in that space.

I think what frequently saved Ali was that he knew almost every musician in town, and they dug him. By that I mean they got him as well as liked him. Ali was a painter, but more to the point, Ali was an artist with his life. Moreover, when Ali was in the house, he could really get a crowd moving and both the musicians and the management appreciated that.

We both knew the band. They knew us, as well. They were in the middle of a number when Ali entered like a storm. "Man, you guys soundin' grand tonight! These are my boys, Bill."

I nodded to the band and they tipped instruments towards us both. We found a table up right up front. A waiter came over and got us some drinks. Ali was up dancing almost immediately. Within five minutes, the whole place was focused on him. He had taken it over, become the spirit of the night, the conductor of the fates. All was cool and easy, at first. Still, the boss of the joint had a look on his face like a ship's captain before a storm. He'd seen this kind of energy turn into a mess many times before.

When the band took a break, a few of them came over to talk to Ali and me. That probably kept the management at bay for awhile.

During the second set, Ali got up and started dancing real close to the musicians when they were playing a solo. I'd seen him do this before. He'd go up to within a foot of the end of the horn or sax; he'd hover near the drums; he'd bend his head down to the sound holes of the bass and groove on the pure, mainlined sound. I've never known anyone who channeled music the way Ali did. I think it penetrated his body as a physical substance. I believe that it entered his bloodstream and then coursed throughout his cells. I think it mingled with and strengthened his soul, which is why he danced so well. When he got closer to the source of the sound, I guess he just got a bigger dose.

I know it had to make musicians nervous, even if they did love him. On the other hand, he usually got them so excited through his infectious dance, that they ratcheted the music up to an even higher plane. Horns did things that they only do in the movies. The bass player doubled-down on his lead and went walking that lonely path that only they know. The drummer became transcendent, syncopathic and LOUD.

That was the breaking point for management. The boss came over and told Ali he had to leave. Ali wasn't happy. In his mind, all he was doing was having a good time. For a few moments, he argued with the owner, as the band settled back down into the lower stratosphere. The bartender and a bouncer came over, and the three of them herded Ali over to the bottom of the stairs.

By this time on the night, I had finally caught up with Ali on drinks, and I didn't want to leave either. More to the point, this was bullshit. No eviction was warranted, so I started arguing with them. Then they kicked me out, too! As we started up the stairs, I was pissed. I was hot and I was raising my voice. I'd forgotten about Ali and everything else around me.

Then I felt a hand on my shoulder. Ali turned to me and said,

"C'mon, Bill. Let it go. They're just doin' their job. Don't give them such a hard time."

Suddenly I was the trouble-maker. Me, the professional guy who knew something like this was going to happen from the get-go. Me, the guy who considered blowing off Ali's birthday all together, because things could often just go wrong when the night was going so good! I started arguing with Ali!

He put his arm around my shoulders, and escorted me up the rest of the stairs and then out into the clean, night air.

"We had a great evening, Bill," he said. "We don't want to spoil the night, do we?"

I laughed.

He had me there.

Suicide Watch

My phone rang one afternoon a few years back. It was a rare call from Ali. Although he always seemed to have a cell phone, it was almost always suspended.

"Hey Bill." Before I could answer he added, "Bill, I've got a big favor to ask."

"Sure, Ali. Name it."

"Bill, I'm in the hospital over here at University of Tennessee."

"Man, Ali, I didn't know you were in the hospital. What for?"

"Well, Bill, I might have told you that I've been having trouble with my neck for a long time. I've been avoiding the recommended surgery, but they finally convinced me I should get it done. It involves a surgery going in the front of my neck to get to the portion of my upper spine they need to fix. I had the surgery three days ago. They released me the same day and gave me some pain pills. Everything was okay at home for a few hours until the anesthesia wore off. Then it got so painful I couldn't stand it. I couldn't sleep at all that night.

"Finally I went back to the hospital and insisted they check me back in. I had to argue with them but they finally admitted me. They've got me on pain medication, but it isn't doing much good. I'm in the worst pain of my life"

"Ali, that sounds horrible. What can I do for you?"

"It gets worse, Bill. I've been arguing with them about it and I was in such pain that one moment in complete exasperation I said, 'What do I have to do to get some attention around here, kill myself?'

"That's when they put me on suicide watch.

"Bill, there's a person sitting in my door now, twenty-four/seven. I can't even go to the bathroom without the door being open. I don't know if you know this, Bill, but I'm a private person. I can't go to the bathroom with someone watching me."

He sounded desperate.

"What can I do, Ali?"

"It's simple, Bill. I need you to put on your best suit and tie and come over here to visit with me. I need a white, professional-looking guy to visit me to show them that I'm not just a dumb black guy. Believe me, once they get that idea in their head there's nothing a black man can do to change it—except maybe show them that I have white friends.

So Bill, get dressed and come over here to see me for a couple of hours."

I was off work that day, so I started changing.

I visited him in his room for a while. Then we walked around the halls, Ali dragging his saline solution behind him. We walked the floor about three times. He said hello to all the nurses and doctors in a very friendly way, sometimes introducing me. After a couple of hours, I left him.

He called me later in the evening.

"Bill, thanks for coming over. They took me off suicide watch. I should get out of here tomorrow."

"That's great, Ali!"

"Goddamnit, Bill! I told you it would work!"

Busted

My friend, Ali Akbar, often had run-ins with the police and other people that got him in trouble. It wasn't that he was a trouble-maker, although those who got on his wrong side probably wouldn't agree. And he wasn't always innocent, either. He did have a penchant for carrying on grudges way beyond a reasonable expiration date. But if he thought he was being wrongly accused of something, or he thought he wasn't being treated with proper respect, he usually called the person out on it. Immediately! And he didn't pull his punches either.

I was talking with my friend Birgitta on the phone one day. "Hey, did you know Ali was in jail?" she asked. We were both friends with Ali. In fact, I had met Ali at Birgitta's house the first time back in about 1997.

"No, what the hell for?" I said.

"Well, I'm not sure what happened but I think

it has something to do with disorderly conduct," she said.

"Disorderly conduct" usually means the person arrested dared to question the cop's behavior. That was usually the reason Ali got in trouble with the law.

"I'll try to find him, and bail him out," I told Birgitta.

After many calls I finally reached Ali in the jail.

"What the hell are you doing in jail, Ali?" I greeted him teasingly.

"Oh hey, Bill. Not for any good reason that's for sure!" he said. He sounded incensed. "They're not goin' to make me take their shit quietly, I'll tell you that!" he said.

"How long you in for?" I asked.

"Ten damn days, Bill! But I've already been in two, so I'll be out in eight."

"Well look, Ali, I'll find out what the bail is and get you out."

"DON'T BAIL ME OUT, BILL!" he shouted. "I'm stayin' in here the whole time. I'm going to eat everything they put in front of me, and I'm askin' for seconds. I swear I'm gonna gain ten god damn pounds while I'm in here. And I'm gonna have a ball too. I've already met just about everyone, and we're having a good time. We're playing cards, telling stories, eating, and sleeping as much as we want. By God, Bill, I'm going to make them pay for arresting me! I intend to get my money's worth in grub and fun the next eight days. So, don't worry about me, Bill. Thanks for the offer, but please *don't* bail me out."

I saw him about two weeks later, and he did seem to have gained some weight.

Ali was frequently in trouble with the law or being kicked out of bars. He didn't start fights or cause trouble in the usual ways. It was often because his behavior was out of the ordinary, like dancing or raising his voice in joy. When asked or nudged into the status quo, he wasn't going to go quietly. With the cops it was the same. He didn't try to fight them, but he *was* going to question them. As we all know, they don't like that.

Ali was probably kicked out of every bar in town at some time or another. He had a particularly hard time with a downtown watering hole. I was always surprised he would go back there, but I think he just liked the place in general.

He told me this story one day:
    "One late afternoon I was there at that bar, sitting in a booth drinking a few beers. I was downtown

for some reason, and I like to drop in there every once in a while. You know, Bill, I just dig the place. I didn't see anyone I knew, so I sat by myself. I got up to leave. I was carrying a large shoulder bag. I got almost to the door when I heard a yell behind me, 'He's stolen my purse!' some woman shouted.

"I didn't know who she was referring to. I went out the door, but I heard a commotion behind me. 'He's the one,' she hollered to the bartender, pointing at me. I turned around. They had both followed me out the door. By now, I was standing just outside the patio area.

"'I don't know what the hell you're talking about,' I said.

"More people came out from the door. There must have been ten people standing looking at me.

"'Sir, can I look in your bag?' the bartender said.

"'Hell no, you can't look in my bag.'

"The woman said, 'He was sitting in the booth behind me, and he must have taken my purse when I wasn't looking.'

"'I didn't take nuthin' from nobody', I said.

"'We're calling the police if you don't let us look in your bag,' the bartender said.

"I looked at them all: her, the bartender, the crowd. There wasn't a friendly face among them. They looked hostile. I was pissed. But in my mind I was making a calculation. I knew I hadn't stolen her purse. But I knew if the police came I was goin' to jail anyway because I knew I'd mouth off. I just wasn't into goin' to jail right then.

"'OK, you fuckers, I'll show you my bag.'

"I wouldn't let them look in it. Instead I walked right through that mob and into the bar. I went up to the nearest table. They all followed me. I dumped the entire contents of my bag on the table.

"'Are you satisfied?'

"Then I let them have it!

"'You bunch of sons of bitches! Not one of you, not one, gave me the benefit of the doubt. You all stood by and watched while I was accused for no other reason than that I guess I was the only black guy in there. I feel sorry for all of you. You're a bunch of hypocrites and cowards.'

"I saw the bartender go over to the woman's booth and fish her purse out from under the bench.

"I didn't even give them time to apologize. I just put my stuff back in my bag and walked out."

But an incident like that usually just rolled off Ali's back. He'd be in that bar again within a week, with no chip on his shoulder whatsoever.

He told me about another episode in the same bar just a few months before he died:

"Bill, I had another problem at that same bar a week ago. Man, I don't know what it is about that place that gets me in trouble."

"What happened?" I asked.

"It was like this. I wandered down one afternoon and dropped into that same bar to see if there was anyone I knew. Hell, everyone I know drinks there! Just as I got there I ran into an old friend. I hadn't seen her or her husband in years. She was alone, but she said he was coming to meet her in about an hour.

"We sat down in the patio. I said I'd buy her a beer while we waited. You know, Bill, that I stopped drinking about a month ago. After that trip we took to DC, and how much we drank up there, I felt I had to pull back a little. So, I went in to buy the beer. I went up to the bar and ordered it. It was in the afternoon. It wasn't crowded. The bartender, a woman, poured the beer and I gave her my credit card. I didn't have any cash on me. She asked if I wanted to start a tab. I didn't intend to stay, so I said 'No, just put it on the card.' She gave me a sour look, but ran the card.

"Later, my friend's husband came, and we were excited to see each other. They begged me to stay and talk for awhile. I said I'd buy them a beer. I went in again to the bar. The same bartender came up to me. I ordered the beers. She brought them to me and asked if I wanted to start a tab. I said, 'No, I'm not staying. This is all I'm having.' I gave her my card. She gave me a dirty look and went to run the card. She was getting my goat.

"When she came back with the card, she said in a very nasty way, 'This is the last time I'm running your card. If you don't start a tab I'm not going to serve you!'

"I said, 'I don't really give a shit whether you ever serve me again, bitch!'

"Whoa, she got pissed. She demanded I give her back the beers. I told her I'd already paid for them and I wasn't giving them back.

"As I walked away, I heard her yelling to the other bartender, 'Call the police!'

"'Heeere we go,' I thought.

"I walked out to the patio to deliver the beers to my friends. Here come the bartenders following me, her screaming at me, 'Give me those beers back!'

"My friends just looked up at me wondering what the hell could have happened in such a short time.

"I was standing there with the beers still in my hand. She was screaming to give them back. The other bartender was saying he had called the police. I didn't want to go to jail. She was standing right in front of me, still yelling. I slowly turned both glasses over, spilling the entire pints on the patio, splashing all over her and my feet. Then I calmly put the glasses down on a table, said good-by to my friends, and walked away.

"Bill, I got some bad luck in that bar!"

That Means You Love Me

Once at about one in the morning, I was sitting around the house after having just returned from some bar. I was feeling okay—not too drunk, but not sleepy either.

My cell phone rang. It was Ali.

"Ali, wassup?"

No answer.

"Hey Ali, what's going on?"

No answer.

All I could hear was a sort of groan and the voices of other people.

I tried shouting!

Nothing.

I do have a healthy imagination, I'll admit. The thought crept into my mind that he was in some kind of trouble.

Maybe having a stroke. But whose voices? I wondered.

I listened closer. Was that laughter?

"Oh, shit . . ." I thought. "Did he get knocked down at some party?" That was always a possibility with Ali.

I didn't want to hang up, so I went to Chris's room and knocked. He was asleep.

"Uhrh?" he responded.

"Hey Chris, sorry to wake you. I got a little issue going on."

I explained. He listened.

Back on the phone, there were still occasional groans and multiple voices in the background.

I asked Chris to call Ali on Chris's phone hoping Ali had call-waiting. The line was busy.

We talked about it. He didn't have any better idea what to do than me.

"You know he's in bad health. Should we call for help?"

Chris hesitated. We both knew how much Ali hated the building management and the cops.

I didn't know what else to do, so I called 911 on Chris's phone while keeping mine on with Ali. I couldn't remember his address or room number, but they knew which public housing unit it was.

I didn't want to lose the connection, so I didn't hang up Ali's call.

I sat down to wait. I had worked myself into a nervous state. I couldn't sit anymore, so I decided to drive over to Ali's place. I kept the phone to my ear.

I got about halfway there when I heard knocking on a door.

"Heh?"

More knocking. Much louder.

"Whass?"

I heard the door opening and then Ali's voice:

"WHAT THE FUCK? WHO THE FUCK ARE YOU GUYS? AND WHAT THE FUCK ARE YOU GUYS DOING IN MY APARTMENT?"

"Oh, shit!!!" I thought.

I hung up the phone and turned the car around.

Once home I told Chris what had happened. He had the same reaction, "Oh, shit!!!"

I waited about half an hour. Then I called Ali.

"Hey Bill, wassup?"

He sounded chipper.

"What you doing, Ali?" I asked.

"Oh, nothing much Bill. Just standing outside enjoying the evening."

"It was me," I confessed. "I called them."

"What?"

I repeated, "I called them.' I'm the one who called the ambulance."

"YOU CALLED THE GODDAMN AMBULANCE? I ALMOST GOT ARRESTED FOR CREATING A DIS-TURBANCE! WHY IN THE HELL DID YOU CALL THEM???" he shouted.

Surprisingly, he managed to do it without seeming mad.

"BECAUSE YOU POCKET-CALLED ME, YOU ASSHOLE!!! I THOUGHT YOU WERE HAVING A STROKE!!!"

There was a long pause.

"Man, Bill, that's sweet. That means you love me!"

"What was all the talking I could hear?"

"That was just the TV, Bill. I was drunk, and I guess I fell into bed with my phone in my pocket . . . You know what, Bill? I'm feeling pretty good. I think I'm gonna go find one more beer."

Two Fingers

"Bill, I think this is the time," said Herbie. He was calling me from DC, where he lived. "We've been talking about doing this for five years now, and none of us is getting any younger." He was talking about our idea for me to drive Ali up to DC for a long weekend visiting with Herbie. He was right. We had originally thought of it close to five years ago when Herbie first met Ali in Knoxville, and hit it off with him so well. Herbie is my oldest and best friend. We've known each other for more than 40 years.

"I've got a long weekend coming up Labor Day. I'll have Friday and Monday off," he continued. "There's some great art shows at the Smithsonian and elsewhere that are on now, and then we've got Twins and Columbia Station for jazz, and whatever else we can find. You know Ali will love it all."

"You're right," I agreed. "We can't put it off any longer. I'll give him a call and see it he's up to it." Ali's health was going downhill. He had been diagnosed with diabetes earlier in the year. He'd had some dizzy and fainting spells that had landed him in the hospital, and he was having a lot more trouble walking. And he didn't have any health insurance, except for the VA facilities about 100 miles away.

But he was up for the adventure. "Oh man, Bill, that sounds like a blast. You, me, and Herbie, running around Chocolate City for a whole weekend. I'm in!"

"Fantastic, Ali! Let's plan to drive up there on Thursday," I said. "We should get there just about time to meet Herbie after work."

"Now, Bill, you know I probably can't keep up with you guys walking all over the place," he cautioned.

"Don't worry about that Ali," I said. "Herbie knows DC like the back of his hand. He knows every street, shortcut, monument, and bus and subway schedule from memory. And we'll have my car too," I assured him. To my knowledge Herbie has never owned a car. I've never known anyone more at ease on his feet in a big city.

I picked Ali up at his crib early on Thursday morning. He was sitting out front of his low-income, high-rise waiting for me. I couldn't believe the pile of luggage that was sitting next to him. He had two large suitcases, a folded suit wardrobe, and a small bag of shoes.

"What the hell," I kidded him. "You planning on staying longer than the weekend?"

"Now, Bill, you know I like to dress for the occasion," he shot back. "And we don't know what kind of occasions are going to present themselves this weekend. And besides, this is Chocolate City we're going to. Those blacks know how to dress. I don't wanna look like no country bumpkin."

It was a great day for a long drive.

The temperature had cooled down to the lower 80's, so we could drive with the windows open. The sky was wonderfully blue. I brought along a good sample of music, from blues to jazz and some world music mixed in as well. Plenty to dig on for the eight-hour drive up I-80.

As we approached DC, we got to talking about Obama's election just a year ago. I hadn't ever asked Ali what he thought about that.

"Bill, I really didn't pay much attention to the election. I was damn certain America was not goin' to elect no black man as president, and I sure didn't want to set myself up for a big disappointment." Ali continued, "When he won, I wasn't prepared for it. I simply couldn't believe it. It's a milestone."

"I know what you mean," I said. "I kind of had the same idea. I didn't even want him to run in the primary, because I felt it would be hopeless for him to win the presidency." We both became silent thinking that over.

Then Ali said very seriously, "Bill, I'll tell you what the biggest thing is about that election."

"What's that, Ali?", I said expecting some novel insight into American politics and culture.

"*Black men goin' to get a lot more white pussy now,*" he exclaimed, laughing and slapping his hand down hard on his leg!

I never knew what was going to come out of his mouth next.

"OK, fine, I said, not wanting him to have the last word. "Well, what that means is there's going to be a lot of lonely black women around, and some of us white guys might just move in on that opportunity."

"Sure, Bill, that's fine," he conceded, laughing and dismissing me, still enjoying his joke.

We rolled into DC just after the rush hour. We headed up to Herbie's apartment near 16th & U, NW. It's a sweet location, just a couple of blocks in either direction to two great entertainment districts. 14th and U was a famed black entertainment district during the early 20th century. It was named Washington's Black Broadway by some. Duke Ellington was born there. It suffered decline in the 1970's, but now there has been a significant redevelopment. It's home to a number of good jazz clubs including our favorite, Twins. Three blocks to the west is the Adams Morgan district, along 18th street. It has more of a college-age and world feel with many ethnic restaurants and clubs.

Herbie and I always go to Madam's Organ, a tiny but lively bar in the Adams Morgan district on Thursday night. The Patrick Alban and Noche Latina band has played a weekly gig on Thursday night for well over 10 years. They play an eclectic and rocking blend of world, Latin, and blues—fantastic dancing music. We knew Ali would dig it. Ali was considered one of the best dancers in Knoxville. Even Patti Smith gave him a nod one night for his dancing at her show in front of the stage. That is, until the management asked him to sit down. We headed up there about 9pm. It was a warm, wonderful night walking down U Street. We were all feeling excited about the weekend.

The band didn't let us down. It didn't take long for Ali to get up dancing. You wouldn't know from his dancing that he was having trouble getting around on his feet. I was up dancing myself not long after; their music is that infectious. As I mentioned, the place is tiny. There's only a smallish bar along one side, a few stand-up tables along the other side, and a completely open area in the middle which quickly fills with dancers. Ali moved to just in front of the band, where he usually liked to be.

Somehow in the mix of the dance floor I found myself dancing with a beautiful black woman. You
know how that goes. The dance floor is tight. You're
dancing by yourself. You turn and there she is dancing by herself. A friendly, inviting smile and you're
dancing together. The music stops momentarily.
She doesn't walk away. You introduce yourself. The
music starts again and there you go. She said her
name was Awa. She was from Mali. She was tall and
shapely. She had a wonderful smile. I danced with
her for a long time, and lost track of Herbie and Ali.

When the band took a break, I took Awa upstairs
to talk. She said she only stopped in Madam's for
a moment because she was in town to see a friend
who was going to play up the street. She told me
her friend was a great banjo player from Mali. I
later learned she was talking about Cheick Hamala
Diabaté, Malian musician and griot, a sort of song
storyteller in African culture. He had toured and
collaborated with Bela Fleck, famed banjo player
from the US.

She needed to leave to go see him. I asked her if
I could call her. She gave me her number.

I got the third degree when I returned to Herbie
and Ali. They had seen it all. I blew it off as just
being in the right place at the right time. But I knew
I was going to try that number before the weekend
was over.

The next morning we rolled out of bed.

Herbie made breakfast, which is always fried eggs and grits. He and Ali typically got a kick out of kidding me about grits. Herbie grew up in Memphis and Ali in South Carolina. I'm the Yankee. Whenever I said anything about it they just started singing, "Grits ain't groceries, and Mona Lisa was a man."

Ali came out of his bedroom wearing a robe. "You brought a robe?"

"Bill, I told you I like to be prepared," he bull-shitted back. "Let me show you some of what I brought." He opened one of the suitcases. There was a box with five identical, but different colored hats: white, black, red, blue, yellow. I'd seen that box before. He found it at a thrift store on his way to my house one day. He was damned excited about those hats. "You see these hats? I've got an outfit with me that works with each one of those colors!" And he did. We saw each one of them that weekend.

We spent the morning listening to Herbie's blues and jazz LP collection and listening to the many blues/jazz radio stations Herbie has programmed into his computer. "Hey, it's 11:30, that's time for the Blues Show on WWOZ out of New Orleans," Herbie said. He must have at least ten programs a week memorized.

I gave Awa a call. She didn't answer. I left a message.

Sometime around noon we took off walking. Ali was feeling his oats. He talked to everyone. We were walking to the car, parked in Herbie's neighborhood. A young black man pulled up to a stop sign beside us. Ali glanced at him. Then, "Man, you dressed fine today!" The guy looked startled, with just a hint of apprehension. We were just feet from him. "Look at that hat, and the way it matches your shirt," he continued excitedly. The guy started smiling. "You going to have a good day with the ladies!" The guy was laughing as he pulled away.

It was like that all day, all weekend. He engaged with just about everyone who came within five feet of us. Women, men, old, young, black, white, police, office workers. . . he was on fire. He was particularly impressed with the blackness of downtown DC. "Man, this is great to see so many black people well dressed, professional, and acting like this is their town. Almost makes me wish I had moved here years ago!"

We drove down to the National Mall Friday afternoon to tour a few museums. We hit a lot of them over the next few days. Ali particularly liked the new African Museum of the Smithsonian and the Hirshhorn Sculpture Garden. He was blown away by the Burghers of Calais, by Rodin.

Afterwards, the three of us were sitting on a park bench along a shady walkway nearby. A nice-looking older black woman walked by in front of us. We all had our eyes on her. Ali hmmmed out, "My, you lookin good!" Herbie and I cringed a little, expecting a disapproving stare. She walked on another few yards, then stopped and turned around. We were still staring at her from the park bench, Ali at the end closest to her, me in the middle, Herbie on the end with our heads pushed forward so we could see past each other. We must have looked like those three famous monkeys except we all had our eyes wide open. She flashed us the biggest smile, and walked away, but not before taking a short glance at her backside to certify that, indeed, she was looking good.

Later that day we headed to a jazz concert at the Westminster Presbyterian Church in one of the traditional, working-class, black neighborhoods in Southwest DC, not too far from the Mall. Herbie had discovered this concert a few years back. It's every Friday night from 7-9 pm. The jazz band is up on the altar; soul food dinner is in the basement.

When we first started going to it we were two of just a few white people there. But that didn't matter much because we fit right in with the age range, over 50. Funny how the older you get, the more

comfortable you feel with people of your own age regardless of race, ethnicity, or gender. They always treated us well, even though we weren't dressed to the nines like everyone else out for that weekly social event.

Ali dug the scene. He jumped right in, jiving the men about their clothes, and flirting with the women. We had the soul-food dinner, and then grabbed ourselves a seat upstairs. The place is always packed. We landed some nice seats right up front. Ali always liked to be near any band so he could more easily show them his appreciation with lots of "Oh man" or "Diggin it!" or "Talk to us!" His comments rarely failed to enliven the band. Musicians love feedback.

We stayed for the whole concert and left with the crowd. We had plans to hit Twins Lounge in Herbie's neighborhood later that evening. Lots of people were talking to Ali. When we got a little way down the sidewalk out of hearing range of the others, he turned to Herbie and me and said seriously, "I just want to tell you guys that prejudice exists on our side too."

"What do you mean, Ali?" Herbie asked. "Everyone there always treats us well."

"I'm not going to tell you what I know, but I am telling you some of them may be friendly and polite to your face, but I can see when they're expressing some prejudice or let's just say stereotyping you. It's not mean, but it ain't too nice either."

He wouldn't elaborate. We let it drop. Ali was a sensitive guy. He picked up on a lot of stuff that other people didn't see.

The next day, Saturday, was a repeat of Friday. Easy-going morning; then off to some more museums and monuments. We hit Twins Lounge for dinner and an early show. It's Ethiopian owned and the dinners are great. The jazz quartet was top notch as usual. Later we closed down another jazz club.

I called Awa again. Same as before; no answer. I left a message that I'd like to see her again.

By Sunday, I had just about given up on ever hearing back from Awa, when she called. That surprised me. She asked if I wanted to visit her that afternoon, Sunday, about two. It wasn't exactly the date I was looking for, but why not? I said I'd drive out there to see her. She lived a little north, but still within the DC suburbs.

She lived in a middle-class apartment complex. I called her from the parking lot. She said she'd come out to the car. She looked as good as I remembered her from Thursday night. She gave me a big hug. Then she asked if I would mind running a little errand with her to deliver some African dresses she had made for a customer. I agreed.

We talked as I drove. She was easy to talk with in spite of the fact that English was her third language. Her first language was Malian, and she was educated in French. We had a lively conversation going on about her dress-making, her life since she left Mali, my life in Tennessee, and more. At one point she turned to me and teased, "How you know I not kidnap you?" I replied, laughing, "How you know I not already kidnap you?" I liked her sense of humor.

We met the customer in a parking lot somewhere. She was another African woman. They took some time looking over the dresses. They were beautiful. Awa introduced me. The other woman seemed mildly curious about me. She was friendly and polite. As we were driving away I mentioned that her friend seemed a little surprised by my presence. "No," she said, "she know I like white men." Step one accomplished, I thought to myself!

Awa asked me what I wanted to do next. I suggested we go somewhere to eat. "What kind of restaurant you like?" she asked. I thought about that, and then suggested, "Why not some African food?"

"If you want African food, we no go to restaurant. I cook Malian food, better than any restaurant." "We go buy food, and then you come to my apartment. I cook for you."

"Sounds great to me," I said.

"Will you buy food?" she asked.

"Of course!"

First stop was a vegetable market where she bought a load of vegetables, fruit, rice and millet, and spices. The market even had cassava root, a staple of many African dishes. She seemed to know exactly what she was after. I was slightly nervous about the arrangement of me buying. I wasn't sure what I was getting into. But the purchases seemed reasonable.

Next stop was a butcher shop. It was the real thing. All kinds of meat. She ordered about ten pounds of lamb and chicken. "Whoa," I thought, "she's planning a feast."

We had to wait. There seemed to be a lot of Africans in the place. One tall guy in a long, decorated African robe and Kufi cap came in. He exhibited a regal bearing, like he was a king. He went up to the young black American kid who was working behind the counter. "I want ten chickens, skinned," he demanded in a forceful voice.

The young guy replied, "I'm sorry sir, we don't skin our poultry."

The king raised his voice, "I want skinned. You know how to skin?" he asked condescendingly. The kid started to object again, but not before the king repeated, a little louder, "I order ten chickens, skinned. You want I talk to boss?" The kid told him to wait a minute, and went looking for the boss. He came back and asked the king what else he'd like to order.

We watched this while leaning against a horizontal freezer against the wall. We got the meat and left. She said we had one more purchase to make. We went to a Big Lots. She bought a bunch of plastic containers. I didn't know what that was about. That was it. We headed to her place.

She took everything to the kitchen as soon as we got in. There were a lot of groceries. I could tell it was going to take some time to cook all of it. But first she needed to call and invite some friends over for the dinner. That done, she got busy in the kitchen. She wouldn't accept any help I offered. Instead, I just stayed in the kitchen and talked with her while she cooked.

People started arriving. They were all Malian. One was newly arrived today from Mali. He was dressed in an African robe. The biggest surprise was that Cheick Hamala Diabaté showed up as well. I had a long conversation with him about his music. He was a little surprised to hear I knew about him, but I explained that Bela Fleck, old-time banjo music, and world music were pretty big in Knoxville, Tennessee.

Finally, there were two other guys who arrived. Everyone spoke French or Malian. I was kind of left out of the conversation, but I was digging the moment anyway. One of the guests turned to me and said, "Why you no in kitchen? Awa want you there." I returned to the kitchen and watched her cook. She was lovely to behold.

It was a fantastic meal. Meat, African vegetables, great sauces, rice, couscous, plantains, lots more. There had to have been five or six different dishes. We ate for well over an hour. In the end, she put all of the leftovers in those containers she bought and gave them to me. She had it all planned. I had no complaints.

I left Awa's about 10 pm. I drove back into DC. The car was filled with the powerful aroma of the leftovers. They were still warm. I wanted to find Ali and Herbie. I had a pretty good idea I would find them at Columbia Station in Adams Morgan. It's a small jazz club, often open-mic. It's right on 18th street in the heart of the strip, surrounded by loud, hip discos and restaurants. It's like an oasis in the heart of urban madness. There are big plate glass windows all across the front. It's great to watch the weekend revelers passing by in a throng while you're grooving inside to jazz refrains. We had already spent a late night there on Friday, and then again on Saturday afternoon. We were already known. The bartender, Akmal, a young man from Uzbekistan, seemed to really enjoy our drunken antics, and how much we dug the music. We tipped him well, too.

My friends were there. I told them I had a feast waiting in the car, but they were in no mood for leaving the music. We decided we'd just reheat everything once we got back home. They were full of questions about the day. I gave them a little synopsis, but told them I'd give them the whole story back at the apartment.

"Hey, Akmal, get our friend a drink," shouted Ali. "He's way behind." Akmal came over smiling.

"Where were you tonight?" he asked teasingly. "Ali and Herbie have been raising a storm. The band has been enjoying them as much as they've been enjoying the band."

Ali butted in with, "He's been out chasing tail, Akmal. He abandoned Herbie and me. Now he won't even tell us what he got into."

I looked around the bar. Akmal was right. Herbie and Ali were the center of attention.

Later, we headed out. We were walking down 18th to get to the car. The sidewalks were crowded with young people. Ali had on one of those hats: red, cocked back and to the side. His pants were hanging pretty low. He had a wallet chain hanging out of his front pocket. He was looking real "gangsta."

We walked by a group of young girls, surrounded by a bunch of guys. All black. Ali engaged with the girls, "Man, you girls looking good tonight!" They got a kick out of him. "You're looking pretty good yourself, Slick" they replied. That got him going. The girls all crowded around him and were asking him all kinds of questions. He was holding court.

I could tell the young guys were not too happy about the turn of events. They were crowded around each other, too. Complaining. Finally, one of them pushed in between Ali and the girls, and addressed one of them, "Alesha, why you talking to this OLD guy?" he complained.

"OLD guy, old guy," Ali attacked him, insulted. "Who you think you are, you young punk!" The kid took two steps back. His friends were laughing. So were the girls.

"Whoa, old fella, no harm, my bad," he defended, thereby making a bad situation worse.

"You wouldn't know class if it hit you on the head," Ali said. "And you never will." And then he pushed through the guys and started walking away. We were following. He was incensed. He thrust out his chest, tilted his head back, and with an extreme gesture of pride and boast he strutted down the sidewalk. The oncoming crowd parted for him like he was Moses on the shore of the Red Sea.

Ali forgot all about that as soon as I opened the car door and he smelled the feast. "Oh, man," he said. "Let's get home."

When we got back to Herbie's we unloaded the food into some pots and pans for reheating. Like cars, cell phones, TV's, and many other modern conveniences that the rest of us take for granted, Herbie doesn't believe in microwaves. Once we had the food in front of us, I started in on the whole story; the ride, the shopping, the cooking, the guests, Awa and everything. They wanted the details. Herbie did most of the questioning. Ali was unusually quiet.

We had finished, got up from the table, and were about to go into the living room to resume our drinking and listening to records when I said, "Oh, yeah, there's something I forgot to tell you." They turned to me with rapt attention.

I'm still not sure at what point it occurred to me that I had this opportunity to spring a trap on Ali. I knew I hadn't planned it. The trajectory of the joke intercepted the trajectory of the story. I could ignore the impulse or run with it.

"What was that?" Ali asked blandly.

"You know how I told you we were waiting in the butcher shop for our order? And we were leaning against that freezer?"

"Yeah," Ali said, expectantly.

"Well, we were leaning, sitting there right next to each other. She was real close. My leg was right up against hers."

"C'mon, c'mon, Bill, spill it," Ali said.

"So, I put my hand down there between our legs, and started stroking her leg."

"And what did she do then?" Ali asked impatiently.

"She turned to me, smiling, and whispered, 'You no touch me there now. I no wear panties.'"

At that, Ali had had it. He turned to Herbie, and exclaimed, partly in jest, but partly in complete seriousness, "Herbie, why is Bill with a black woman and I'm not?!"

And that's when I hit him with it.

"You do remember what you told me was the biggest, most important result of Obama's election, don't you?"

He looked at me in temporary confusion. Then he got it. He'd been had. He took off his hat, threw it on the floor, stomping on it. "Fuck you, Bill. Fuck you!!" he laughed. "Oh, man, you set me up! Fuck you!"

We sat up drinking, talking, and listening to music half the night.

Ali and I hauled out of DC about noon the next day. It was going to be a long ride back home. We were both a little melancholy about leaving, not to mention thoroughly hung-over. We got to talking about the weekend. Ali seemed profoundly affected by all we had seen and done. He couldn't get over how the black population of DC seemed so natural, and in tune with their environment, their city.

"You know, Bill, we saw some great art this weekend too," he said. "Man, what I keep on thinking is why did I quit making my art? I mean, in particular, my canvas art."

"Well, damn, Ali, there's still time to get back into it," I offered.

"I know, Bill, and I've already decided I'm going to do it. But I just can't get over all the time I wasted in the last ten years. And one last thing, Bill, thanks so much for introducing me to Herbie. What a cool cat!"

He curled up in the front seat against the window and fell sound asleep.

He hardly woke up the whole way home. I was pulling into his parking lot in Knoxville about 9 pm. He woke and said, incredulously, "We're home already?" "Yeah, man, you slept and snored the whole damn way," I jived him. "Oh, sorry about that. Thanks for that great weekend, Bill."

Three months later he was gone. He died alone in his apartment around the first of December.

I was back in DC the next Spring to visit Herbie. I usually visit him at least once a year. Of course, this year was a bit melancholy. We couldn't get over the feeling that Ali was there with us. We speculated continually about how he would have liked that meal, that piece of art, that show. . . and that woman! "Ohh my!" we could hear him saying. By the third day, though, we were getting over the melancholy, and beginning to dig on the memory.

It was Sunday. We realized we had put off going to Columbia Station. We both knew why. We walked over to get a beer in the late afternoon. Akmal the Uzbeck was still there. He was washing glasses behind the bar. When he saw us he flashed a big welcoming smile. He held up three fingers to us with a questioning look on his face. It was clear he was expecting the third friend.

Without thinking we each put up two fingers. We were both somber. His face shifted from happy to concerned. He put down the glass he was washing, dried his hands, and slowly walked over to greet two friends who had returned to toast a departed third.

Twenty Dollars

One day Ali showed up unexpectedly at my house—which was the way he normally would. That was fine. I was always glad to see him. For me anyway; my dog Lilly always seemed to want to bite him. "Damn, Lilly," he'd say with feigned complaint, "why don't you ever remember me?"

After that we went into the kitchen for some coffee. And, just like usual, Ali said, "Bill, I've got a story for you this time. It just happened, too."

"Hit me, Ali."

"Well, I was coming over here on the bus. Shortly after I got on, this beautiful, young black woman got on. Man, Chicago, she was stunning. She sat a little up from me by herself. We were both sitting sideways so I could look at her. I was thinking to myself, 'Now, how can I start up a conversation?'

"After awhile she pulled out her phone and made a call. After she hung up, I said to her, 'That's the same kind of phone I have. Do you like it?'

"Well, that got us talking and I told her I'd never seen her on the bus before. You know, I ride the bus a lot.

"She said, 'No, I'm not from here. I'm from Louisville, Kentucky. I'm only here because my brother was in a terrible auto accident near here and he's in the hospital. I came down with my mother. We don't know anyone here.'

"'Oh, that's terrible,' I said. I could tell she was near tears just talking about it.

"She told me that her brother had near-died twice while in the hospital, and they had no idea whether he was going to make it.

"I moved over to sit beside her. I told her that her brother was in Allah's hands now, and that we can only pray for him to make it through.

"My stop was coming up and I got up to get off. I said goodbye and gave her my blessing. But just before I got off, I dug in my pocket, pulled out a twenty and walked back and gave it to her. She thanked me. It was just down the street, just moments ago."

"Man, Ali, that was nice of you."

"Thanks Bill, I felt so bad for her."

After awhile I told Ali that I had an errand to run for an hour or two. I asked if he wanted to stay and wait for me at the house. He said, "Take me down to Barley's Tap on your way out and then I'll make my way back to your house later."

I dropped him off there.

About three hours later, he showed up back at my house. "You're not going to believe what happened to me now! Right after you dropped me off, I walked into Barley's, sat at the bar, and ordered a Guinness. Just as the bartender was delivering the pint, I heard a guy walking in say to me, 'I know you.'

"I looked at him. I'd never seen him before. He was white, and I thought, 'Here we go, what's going to happen to me now?'"

Ali was always on his guard to what next challenge or complaint was going to end him up in jail.

"Chicago, man, he walked right up to me and said, 'I saw what you did on the bus.'

"'Uh-oh, here it comes . . .' I thought. But before I could respond, he pulled out a $20 dollar bill and handed it to the bartender.

"'That will pay for his drinks today,' he said. Then he walked out."

Ali stood up, excitedly, for emphasis, and said, "See Bill, it only took an hour for that $20 to come back to me!"

About Ali Akbar

Horace Pittman was born in 1945 in the Piedmont region of South Carolina. He was the only student in his senior yearbook to list "artist" as his ambition. Pittman served in the Army, was wounded in Vietnam, and returned to his home town. He arrived in Knoxville, Tennessee shortly after 1982, the year of the Knoxville World Fair.

The World's Fair unleashed an artistic fervor within a group of young, counter-cultural, artists, musicians, and hipsters. Horace, later to recreate himself as Ali Akbar, was welcomed into a group that started creating guerrilla art wherever there was a blank wall. Although he later produced a wide range of drawings and canvas art, more importantly he created himself as Knoxville's walking, jive-talking, dancing Pan, the eternal spirit of art, music, and life.

My original intention in writing down some stories about my friend, Ali Akbar, after his death was solely to make them available to the people in Knoxville who knew him, and would be attending the retrospective art show that we knew we eventually wanted to stage. I was fairly certain that anyone attending that show wouldn't need a description of Ali, because they already knew him. I wasn't sure how to approach the writing of the stories. I decided to let Ali tell his own stories, and in so doing, make known whatever aspects of his life he divulged to me in the course of our adventures together.

I know a lot more about his life now than I did before his death. But for some reason I find myself resisting the idea of giving the reader more of his biography. I think the reason is that now, after writing nine stories about him, I've come to see a universality in his character and his life. He was unique, but he was also an everyman. I hope that comes through for the reader as well. I wouldn't want the mundane specifics of his life, like all our lives, to lessen the impact of that everyman.

Learn more about Ali Akbar:

- *Who Is This Man?* by RB Morris, a poet, singer/songwriter, and long-time friend of Ali will be available soon from RB's publishing company, Rich Mountain Bound. This book will include most of Ali's art and a detailed essay on Ali's life and thoughts.

- Imagerap.net - A website created to commemorate Ali's life and artwork, is a source for viewing and purchasing his art work and reading about his life. It will be interactive so that people will be able to write their own reminiscences about him. We like to think that some folks, years from now, researching Knoxville's past history, might stumble upon this site and say, "Wow, that must have been a gas to have lived then."

- A film, "Artist," directed by David McGowan features nine interviews with various people in Knoxville about their experiences with Ali, and some wonderful video footage shot by Eric Sublett and Rus Harper many years ago. It can be found at Imagerap.net.

About the Author

Bill McGowan is a freelance writer who spends most of the year living in Antigua, Guatemala where he manages an eclectic bookstore, Dyslexia Libros, owned by an equally eclectic dive bar, Café No Sé, where part of his pay is in drinks.

Bill was born in 1947 in Pittsburgh, Pennsylvania and spent a major portion of his life in and around Chicago, Illinois. For the last twenty years he has been based in Knoxville, Tennessee. After retiring in 2007 from a career in government he began traveling and landed eventually in Antigua, Guatemala.

Bill began writing stories of his interactions in the bookstore, personal life experiences, travel adventures, and sketches of people he has known, for *La Cuadra* magazine (lacuadraonline.com), an English language magazine for expats in Antigua. Seven of the stories from this collection about his friend, Ali Akbar, were first published in *La Cuadra* in January, 2013.